To Liz —

The RAINBOW HAND

Poems About
Mothers and
Children

HAND

Rainbows for you!

ALSO BY JANET S. WONG

Good Luck Gold and Other Poems

A Suitcase of Seaweed and Other Poems

Margaret K. McElderry Books

The RAINBOW HAND

Poems About
Mothers and
Children

Janet S. Wong

illustrations by Jennifer Hewitson

Margaret K. McElderry Books

To my mother
and to Glenn's mother
and to the grand mother of this book,
Margaret McElderry
—J. S. W.

For my mother, my guide
—J. H.

Margaret K. McElderry Books
An imprint of Simon & Schuster Children's Publishing Division
1230 Avenue of the Americas
New York, NY 10020

Book design by Nina Barnett

The text of this book is set in Mrs. Eaves.
The illustrations are rendered in scratchboard and watercolor dyes.

Printed in Hong Kong
First Edition
10 9 8 7 6 5 4 3 2 1

Library of Congress Cataloging-in-Publication Data
Wong, Janet S.
The rainbow hand: poems about mothers and children / Janet S. Wong; illustrations by
Jennifer Hewitson.—1st ed.
p. cm.
Summary: A collection of eighteen original poems about mothers and motherhood,
including "Mother's Heart," "Old Mother Chung," and "The Pilot."
ISBN 0-689-82148-4
1. Motherhood—Juvenile poetry. 2. Mother and child—Juvenile poetry. 3. Mothers—
Juvenile poetry. 4. Children's poetry, American. [1. Mother and child—Poetry.
2. Mothers—Poetry. 3. American poetry.] I. Hewitson, Jennifer, ill. II. title.
PS3573.O578R3 1999 811'.54—dc21 97-50554

Contents

Foreword

I love my mother very much—now. When I was young, I liked my father much more than my mother, and I let her know it. Daddy wasn't busy cooking, too busy to play ping-pong with me. Daddy didn't rush off to do the dishes, he told stories. He didn't shampoo my hair, with the water running into my eyes. He never made me clean my room. He was fun.

Now that I am a mother—and not very much fun anymore!—I can see what my mother has done for me. Still, she can drive me crazy the way no one else can. Still, she makes me cry. But each time I wade through my three-year-old's pile of toys, I wonder how my mother kept the house so clean. Each time I hand the whining little guy a piece of candy, I thank her for giving me a piece of fruit she grew herself.

I hope to follow her in the tradition of great mothers. I am glad I did not become a mother too soon, before I had seen a bit of the world. Now I am ready to walk in her shadow, bright with hope.

—J. S. W.

In Mother's Shadow

I walk behind Mother
through the woods
careful
not to touch the poison oak
she points to with her stick.

She sees snakes before
they move.

She finds her way
by the smell of the trees.

She stops to rest
the very moment
my shoes grow
heavy
and gives me water,
gives me shade

in her steady
shadow.

In My Hand

We stand side by side, my mother and I,
dish towels on our shoulders,
palms up to the light.

> *Our heart lines are weak.*
> *Our head lines are strong.*
> *In our family*
> *the life lines run long.*

Her hand looks the same as it always has looked,
but I can see my lines have changed

and one wild crease I've never seen
is settling in this map of skin—

one bold line to mark the place
where my *own* wild life
begins.

The Pilot

My mother works
in our school library
reading poems and stories
in a voice that soars up to the ceiling,
flapping her arms in the air,
flying us around the world

and leaving us there

when the bell rings at three.

I'll find my way back
tomorrow.

White Hairs

I
love my mother's white hairs,
pure white, cut down when she sees them.
They grow back like daisies
poking through dark mulch.

She
tells me to pull these white stubs out
as they reappear on her head
one or two at a time.

So I pluck them
the way you pick a daisy
apart

> *She loves me*
> *She loves me not*

Seven white hairs
so far—

She loves me.

The Rainbow Hand

Look
how the mother loves her baby,
how she holds him
with strong arms,
high,
so the sun
can warm his face,
so his bones will grow straight.

Look how she runs with him,
to send a cool breeze
through his toes,

how she makes
an umbrella
of her arms
when the rain
starts to fall.

And when lightning
flashes bright,
too bright,
see how she slips her hand
over his eyes,
her fingers curved

like a rainbow.

The Rag

Runny nose?
What better rag than Mother's apron,
rich with the smell of lemon soap.

Another mess?
Mother will clean it up.
Don't worry. Leave it. Run and play.

Mother the Rag saves the day.

Smother Love

The boy asks his mother,
"Who will take care of me when you die?"
"I will not die soon," the mother says,
and pats him on his head like a dog.

But the boy wants to know.
"What if you die next month? Next year?"

The boy, so small, has made his mother afraid.

She looks twice before she crosses the street.
She washes her hands ten times a day.
She stops eating duck skin,
standing in front of the microwave.

She holds his hand tight in the market.
She hugs him so hard he cannot breathe.
Red in the face, the boy struggles free from her arms,
shouting, "You trying to kill me?"

Old Mother Chung

Old Mother Chung
took care of her young

so they would grow
strong and wise.

She did not figure
when they grew bigger

they'd bother her
more than flies!

Meat Loaf Again, Mother?

Meat Loaf
Oxtail
Meat Loaf
Roast

Meat Loaf
Corned Beef
Meat Loaf
Ghosts are filling up my dreams at night!
I couldn't eat another bite!

14

Mother, May I?

Mother, may I
take a giant step?

Or two?

> One
> little
> one,
> very small,
> will do.

I'm falling behind!
Look at my friends!

> So you have to do *everything*
> they do, then?

Upset all my plans!
You're mean!
You're so cruel!

> It's the way of the world:
> Mothers rule.

Don't Be So Lazy!

The room will never be clean enough,
as long as there's even a trace of your stuff—

Don't be so lazy! your mother shouts,
the twentieth time this week.

Don't be so lazy! she nags, again.
You're almost grown! When I was ten—

When she was ten, could she have been
such an amazing freak?

The Light

You show things
harsh, for what they are.

Pimples are pimples.
Roses are full of bugs.

Grandmother told me
Leave those roses an hour
under that light—

Bugs can't take the heat.
The roses will bloom.

The Onion

Mother is like an onion,

her golden skin
smooth and soft.

She keeps you strong.
She is good for you.

Sometimes she surprises you
with sweetness—

so you forget
how she makes *you* cry

each time you cut her
with your words.

Mother's Heart

My mother's heart
is a bottle
I want to fill

    with warm milk
    to soothe her hurts

    with honey
    to trap her bitterness

    with a squirt
    of Tabasco—

Shake her up!

Crazy Mother

Crazy.

You are proud of your mother
and tell how she flipped
the giant man
down
on the sidewalk,
all ninety pounds of her
towering over
that rotten bother.

And when the police came
and looked at her
and listened to him—

They could not help
but laugh, like

Crazy.

Mother's Day

Mother's Day morning
and I have no present.
No money.
I walk outside.

Kicking the dirt,
my toe hits a rock.
A smooth speckled oval,
it could be a gargoyle egg.
Or a paperweight.
Stuck in a box,
wrapped in the gold paper
Mother saved from Christmas,
the old tape peeled off,
it looks like a good gift.

She shakes the box, smiling,
while I stare at her hands
untying the ribbon,
tearing the paper,
lifting the lid.
She holds the rock with flat fingers,
like some rotten egg.

Mother walks into the kitchen,
puzzling. She puts a clove of garlic
on her thick round cutting board
and brings the rock down hard.

"A garlic rock," she says,
pulling chunks of garlic
from the broken skin.
"Just what I needed."

The Gift of Breathing Slow

The mother
holds her baby
close
and face to face
gives him
his first gift,
the gift
of breathing
slow.

In.
Out.

She blows
his hair
clean,
like the ocean
flowing in waves
over the shore.

The baby breathes quick
and soft and shallow,
not even enough to make
water ripple.

And so,
again,
the mother tries,
lying warm and still as a summer night,
breathing full as the moon,

in and out,

and soon
the baby is her echo,
breathing slow
and steady and deep—

his breath
tickling
a smile
out
in his sleep.

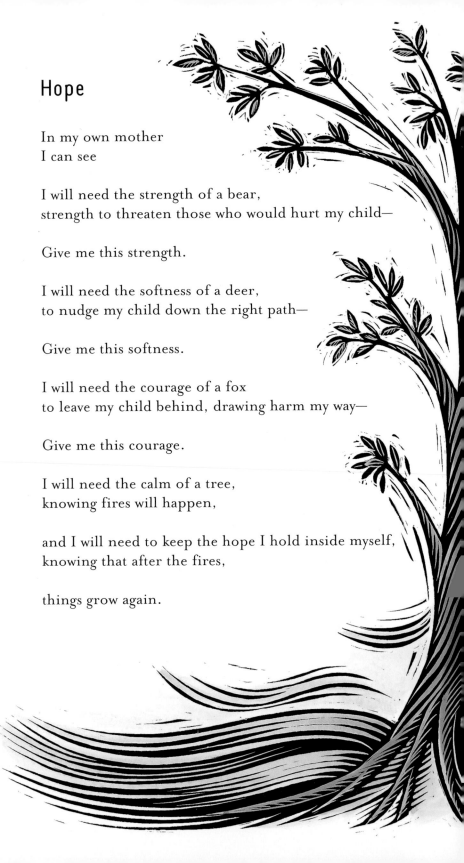

Hope

In my own mother
I can see

I will need the strength of a bear,
strength to threaten those who would hurt my child—

Give me this strength.

I will need the softness of a deer,
to nudge my child down the right path—

Give me this softness.

I will need the courage of a fox
to leave my child behind, drawing harm my way—

Give me this courage.

I will need the calm of a tree,
knowing fires will happen,

and I will need to keep the hope I hold inside myself,
knowing that after the fires,

things grow again.